Please Mr Panda

Steve Antony

Would you like a doughnut?

Give me the pink one.

No, you can not have a doughnut.
I have changed my mind.

Would you like a doughnut?

I want
the blue one
and
the yellow one.

No, you can not have a doughnut.
I have changed my mind.

Would you like a doughnut?

Would you like a doughnut?

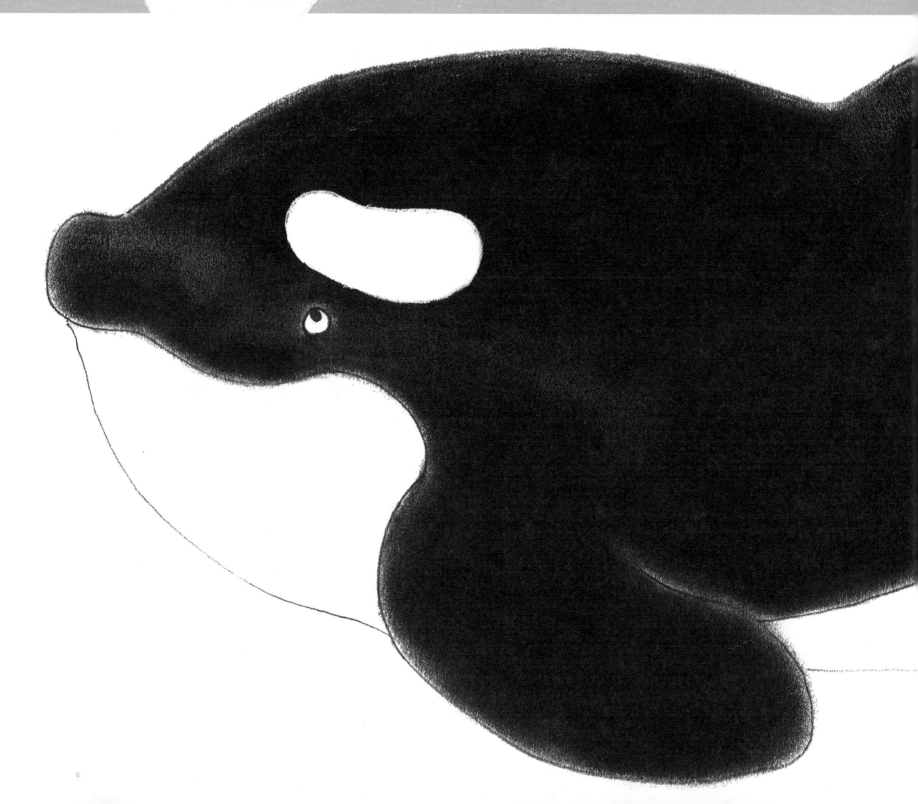

I want them all!

Then bring me some more.

No, you can not have a doughnut.
I have changed my mind.

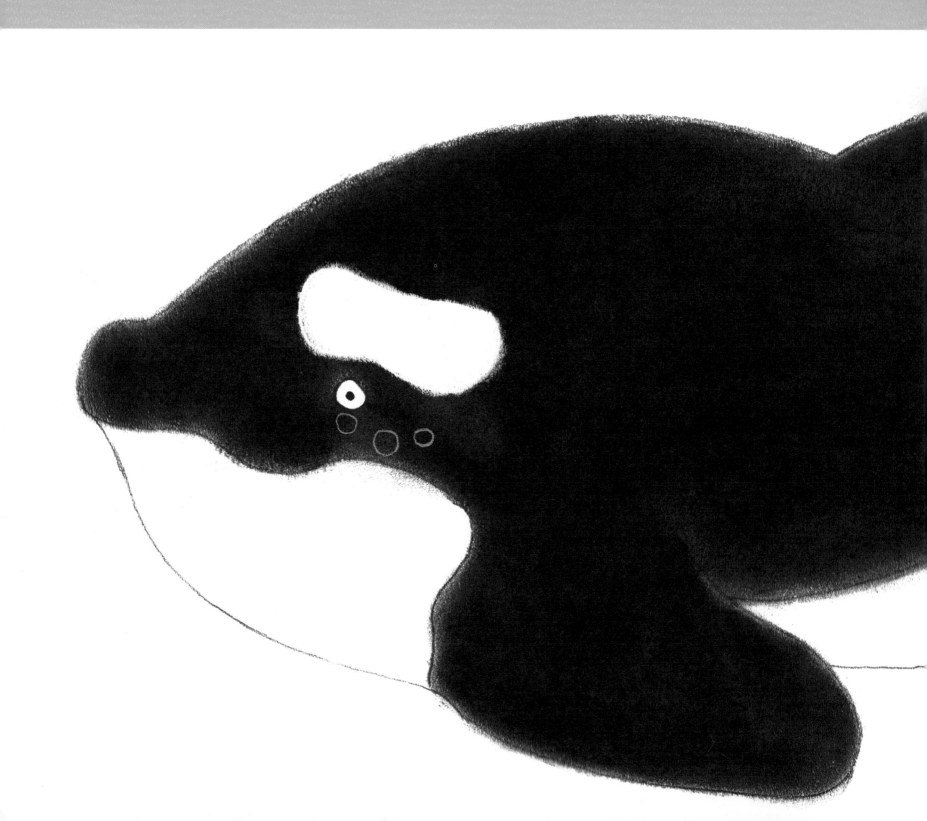

Would anyone else like a doughnut?

Hello!
May I have a doughnut...

Please

Mr Panda.

You can have them all.

Thank you very much!

I love doughnuts.

You're welcome.
I don't like doughnuts.